D0342116

The Mixed-Up Chameleon
by Eric Carle

HarperCollins*Publishers*

*Dedicated to all the children who
have worked with me on this book.*

On a shiny green leaf sat a small green chameleon.
It moved onto a brown tree and turned brownish.
Then it rested on a red flower and turned reddish.
When the chameleon moved slowly
across the yellow sand,
it turned yellowish.
You could hardly see it.

When the chameleon was warm
and had something to eat,
it turned sparkling green.

But when it was cold and hungry,
it turned grey and dull.

When the chameleon was hungry,
it sat still and waited.
Only its eyes moved—up, down, sideways—
until it spotted a fly.
Then the chameleon's long and sticky tongue
shot out and caught the fly.
That was its life.
It was not very exciting.
But one day...

...the chameleon saw a zoo!
It had never seen so many beautiful animals.

ZOO

The chameleon thought:
How small I am, how slow, how weak!
I wish I could be big and white like a polar bear.
And the chameleon's wish came true.
But was it happy?
No!

I wish I could be handsome like a flamingo.

I wish I could be smart like a fox.

I wish I could swim like a fish.

I wish I could run like a deer.

I wish I could see things far away like a giraffe.

I wish I could hide in a shell like a turtle.

I wish I could be strong like an elephant.

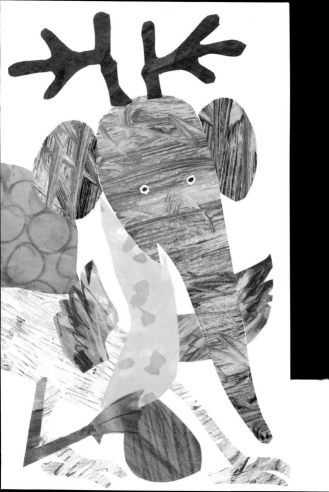

I wish I could be funny like a seal.

I wish I could be like people.
Just then a fly flew by.
The chameleon was very hungry.
But the chameleon was very mixed-up.
It was a little of this and it was a little of that.
And it couldn't catch the fly.

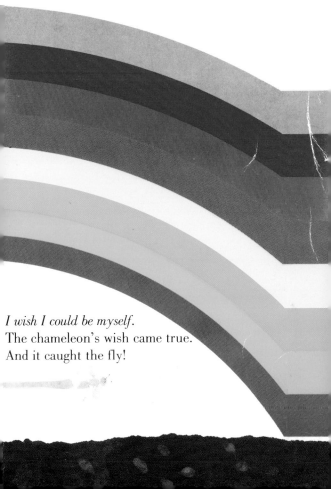

I wish I could be myself.
The chameleon's wish came true.
And it caught the fly!

Eric Carle says that this book had hundreds of co-authors: the children in many schools in all parts of the United States and Europe where the author-artist has visited. "The children are interested to see how a book is made, the technical aspects, from original drawing to printed page. But I always stress that what is more important than the mechanics of production is the idea, imagination, what-you-feel, what-you-think," says Mr. Carle. Together with the children, he "works" on a book about favorite animals. The children make suggestions. Mr. Carle draws. Requests and instructions come in so fast that there is little time to finish drawing an animal. Only the most characteristic parts are drawn. These parts are then strung together. This is how the mixed-up chameleon was born.

Copyright secured 1975, 1984 in countries signatory to International Copyright Union. All rights reserved. Printed in Singapore.
Library of Congress Cataloging-in-Publication Data. Carle, Eric. The mixed-up chameleon / by Eric Carle. — 1st miniature ed. p. cm.
Summary: A bored chameleon wishes it could be more like all the other animals it sees, but soon decides it would rather just be itself. Cutouts along the edges of the pages display various animals and colors.
  1. Toy and movable books—Specimens.   [1. Chameleons—Fiction. 2. Self-acceptance—Fiction.   3. Toy and movable books.]   I. Title.
PZ7.C21476Mi   1991   ISBN 0-06-020103-7   91-2497
[E]—dc20   CIP   AC   First Miniature Edition, 1991